CHICKEN SOUP for LITTLE SOULS

The Braids Girl

Story by
Lisa McCourt

Illustrated by
Tim Ladwig

HCI

Health Communications, Inc.
Deerfield Beach, Florida

Library of Congress Cataloging-in-Publication Data

McCourt, Lisa.
    Chicken soup for little souls : the Braids Girl / story by Lisa McCourt ; illustrated by Tim Ladwig.
       p. cm.
    "Inspired by the #1 New York times best-selling series Chicken soup for the soul."
    Summary: While helping Grandpa Mike do volunteer work at a shelter for less fortunate people, Izzy
tries to figure out the best way to help a girl her own age who is staying there.
    ISBN 1-55874-554-8 (hardcover)
    [1. Homeless persons—Fiction. 2. Poverty—Fiction. 3. Voluntarism—Fiction. 4. Friendship—Fiction.]
    I. Ladwig, Tim, ill. II. Title.
    PZ7.M47841445Cj 1998
    [Fic]—dc21
                                              97-30377
                                            CIP
                                            AC

©1998 Health Communications, Inc.
ISBN 1-55874-554-8

Story inspired by *Chicken Soup for the Soul*®, edited by Jack Canfield and Mark Victor Hansen.

Story ©1998 Lisa McCourt
Illustrations ©1998 Tim Ladwig

Cover Design by Cheryl Nathan

Produced by Boingo Books, Inc.

Publisher: Health Communications, Inc.
               3201 S.W. 15th Street
               Deerfield Beach, FL 33442-8190

Printed in Mexico

Grandpa Mike did volunteer work every Sunday. He called it his "God's Work." I never knew what he meant by that until the Sunday he stopped by our house on his way. "Why don't you come along today, Izzy?" he asked. I'd go anywhere with Grandpa Mike.

We headed off to the Family Togetherness Home, a place where moms and dads and kids stayed when they didn't have any money or anywhere else to live.

Some of the people at the home looked tired and wore strange clothes. It scared me a little bit to be around people who seemed so different from me.

But Grandpa Mike smiled and talked to them all like they were old friends of his. He dished out food for them onto little plastic plates. Sometimes Grandpa Mike pretended he was a waiter in a classy restaurant, serving up fancy meals to important customers. Everybody laughed when he said, "Would Madame care for another biscuit?"

I saw a girl about my age sitting on the floor in the corner. Her clothes were dirty and torn and her hair hung in two long braids that were coming undone because they weren't fastened on the ends. She had her arms wrapped around her bent up knees and she was rocking back and forth with a sad look on her face.

Grandpa Mike saw where I was looking. "Why don't you bring that fine young lady some of this gourmet chowder and sit with her a bit? Looks like she could use some cheering up."

I took the bowl Grandpa Mike handed me and walked slowly toward the girl. What would I say?

When the girl noticed me walking in her direction, she suddenly smiled. "You can eat your soup here by me!" she said super-fast.

Oh no, I thought. *She thinks I live here, too.*

"No! I... uh... brought this for *you*," I stammered. I put it down in front of her and walked quickly back to Grandpa Mike. I tried to look busy serving people food so she would see that I was one of the volunteers. When I looked back at her, she was rocking again with the same sad look.

On the way home, Grandpa Mike said how much he liked having me do God's Work with him. He said I could come any time.

"Why are those people so poor?" I asked him.

"Sometimes people make bad choices and sometimes they just have bad luck," he said. "But we're all God's children, just the same."

I kept thinking and wondering about the girl with the braids. Did she have any other clothes to wear? Did she go to school? Did she ever watch TV? Had she ever been to a movie, or to an amusement park, or even to a museum?

The next day, I called Grandpa Mike. "I want to do God's Work with you again," I told him.

"I'm pleased as punch," he said.

The rest of the week, I gathered up all my outgrown clothes. The Braids Girl was a little smaller than I was, so I guessed they'd fit her fine. I asked Mom if it was okay for me to give my old clothes to a girl I'd seen at the Family Togetherness Home. "I think that's a wonderful idea," she said, hugging me.

It was hard to give up some of my favorite things, even if they didn't fit anymore. My purple high-tops with the beautiful, rainbow-colored laces were the hardest to give away. They were the coolest shoes I'd ever had.

On Sunday, I showed Grandpa Mike the bag of clothes. "I see God's Work agrees with you," he said.

When we got to the Family Togetherness Home, I found the Braids Girl leaning against a woman who must have been her mother.

As I started toward them, I suddenly felt unsure about the bag of clothes in my hands. Would she like the same kinds of clothes I like? Would her mother mind me giving her the clothes?

When the Braids Girl saw me, her whole face lit up. She took a big step in my direction, saying, "You came back!"

"I just wanted to give you these clothes," I said nervously, handing her the bag.

Her smile disappeared. "Thank you," she mumbled.

I hurried over to the other volunteers.

She walked back to her mother and leaned again into her side.

I helped Grandpa Mike the rest of the morning. I saw the Braids Girl looking at me a couple of times, but whenever she saw me looking back, she turned away.

On the way home, I asked Grandpa Mike, "Why didn't the Braids Girl like the clothes I brought her?"

"Oh, I'm sure she appreciated that, Izzy," he said. "But maybe it wasn't what she really needed most."

I thought about that for a few days.

What she really needs are some things of her own, I thought. I spent the rest of the week deciding which of my things I could bear to part with. Some of my stuffed animals had seen me through plenty of sad times. Maybe they would help the Braids Girl feel happier. I had some favorite books, too, that would cheer anyone up. Soon I had a bag full of what I thought were the best choices, including a comb and some hair bands so she could fasten her braids.

Grandpa Mike was happy that I wanted to keep helping him with his God's Work. He said the other volunteers had told him how lucky he was to have such a caring and special grand-daughter. That made me feel good inside. But why didn't the Braids Girl make me feel that way? *She's got to love the stuff I've packed for her now*, I said to myself. But deep down, I had my doubts.

The next Sunday, the Braids Girl skipped over to me before I even had a chance to look for her.

"Do you want to play hopscotch?" she asked, pointing to a hopscotch board she had scratched in the dirt just outside the doorway.

"Um...no," I said, "but I wanted to give you this stuff. I hope you like it."

The Braids Girl looked in the bag and sighed. "Thanks," she said without a smile.

I didn't know what to say so I walked back to Grandpa Mike. It bothered me that nothing I did ever made the Braids Girl happy.

"Why the glum face, Iz?" Grandpa Mike asked.

"I just don't understand," I said. "Every time I give anything to the Braids Girl she looks more sad than she did before. I want to make people happy and do God's Work like you. What am I doing wrong, Grandpa Mike?"

Grandpa Mike knelt down beside me. "Well, first tell me something, Izzy. Why is it that you call that child 'the Braids Girl?'" he asked.

"Because she always wears those unfastened braids," I said, "and I don't know her name."

Grandpa Mike scratched his chin. "Best way I know of to find out a person's name is to ask 'em," he said. "God's Work doesn't have to be hard. In fact, when you're doing it right, it feels just about better than anything." He gave my hand a squeeze, then went back to joking and laughing with the people he had come to serve.

The Braids Girl had changed into my old yellow jumper, but she didn't look any happier than she had looked before. I watched her and thought about what Grandpa Mike had said. Maybe *things* weren't all that she needed. Maybe what she needed most of all couldn't be carried in a bag. I was nervous, but I knew what I wanted to do—what I should have been doing all along.

"Hi," I said. "My name is Isabella. But most everyone calls me Izzy."

The Braids Girl looked up, not sure at first that she could trust me this time. Then she smiled that super-big smile. "I'm Susan," she said.

Susan, I thought, *a real person with a real name.*

"Want to play hopscotch?" I asked her.

"Are you sure?" asked Susan. "You really want to?"

"C'mon!" I said.

After we played, Susan looked in the new bag I had brought her. "How come you keep giving me things?" she asked.

I didn't know what to tell her. In the beginning I had wanted to help her because she was poor. But now... "Because I want to be your friend," I blurted out.

"That's what I was hoping since the first time I saw you!" Susan said.

"I brought these for your braids," I said, taking out the hair bands and barrettes.

Susan fingered her hair shyly. "Maybe, with those—" she pointed to the barrettes— "my hair could be more like yours."

"Sure it could," I said. "I'll show you." I unbraided Susan's hair and combed it out. It hung loose and bouncy down her back. Then I used the barrettes to pull back each side, just like mine.

Susan ran over to a shiny stew pot to see her reflection. She looked pretty and her smile was bigger than ever.

She ran back and surprised me with a soft hug. "You're the nicest girl I've ever met," she said.

Susan and I talked and played games the rest of the morning. We laughed and told secrets and had lots of fun! She told me her mom had gotten a housecleaning job and they were leaving the home the next day to live with a family in my town. She'd even be going to the same community day camp I was going to for the summer. She was a regular kid, just like me and my friends. And that's what she'd wanted right from the start—for me to see her that way.

Later, when Grandpa Mike said it was time to go, I said good-bye to Susan. "I'll save you a seat on the bus on the first day of camp next week," I promised her.

"Wait," Susan said, "I have something to give *you* this time." She reached in her pocket and pulled out a colorful, braided friendship bracelet.

Susan took my arm and tied the bracelet around my wrist. The beautiful colors of the braided string looked familiar. A braided gift from the Braids Girl. Only she would never be just the Braids Girl to me again.

"That's so you'll remember me," she whispered.

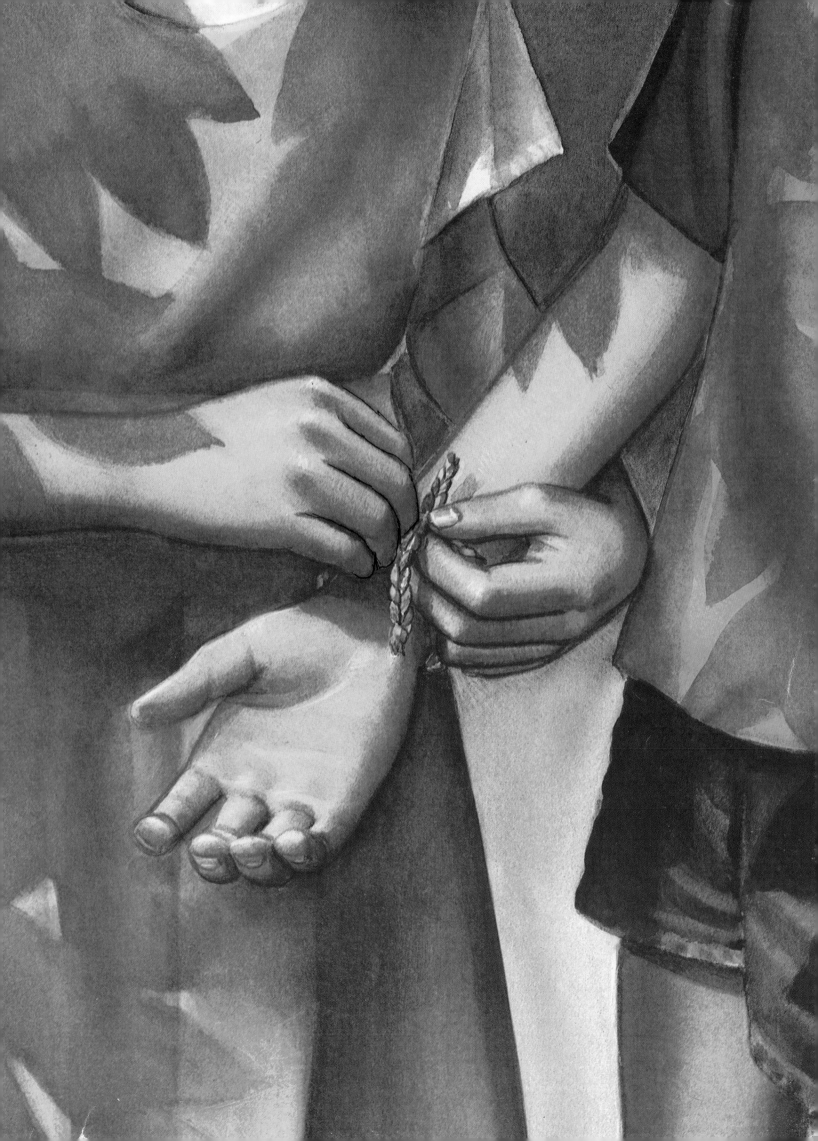

I suddenly knew why the bright colors in the bracelet looked so familiar to me. I looked down at Susan's feet. Sure enough, she was wearing my special outgrown high-tops—except that now they were held together by old, gray-white strings. All she had in the world were the things I had given her, and she had given up the prettiest of those things so she could make a gift for me.

Tears stung in my eyes. "I'll remember you, Susan," I said. "I'll remember you for sure."